SPELLING WICKEDLY WEIRD

THE DARKLING CURSE

CHRIS MOULD

Roaring Brook Press
New York

Text and illustrations © 2008 Chris Mould. First published by Hodder Children's
Books, a division of Hachette Children's Books,
an Hachette Livre UK company.
Published by Roaring Brook Press
Roaring Brook Press is a division of Holtzbrinck Publishing
Holdings Limited Partnership
175 Fifth Avenue, New York, New York 10010
www.roaringbrookpress.com
All rights reserved
Distributed in Canada by H. B. Fenn and Company Ltd.
Cataloging-in-Publication Data is on file at the Library of Congress
ISBN: 978-1-59643-387-8
Roaring Brook Press books are available for special promotions
and premiums.
For details contact: Director of Special Markets, Holtzbrinck Publishers
First Edition August 2009
Book design by MT Dikun
Printed in July 2009 in the United States of America by RR Donnelly & Sons
Company, Bloomsburg, Pennsylvania
10 9 8 7 6 5 4 3 2 1

For Ed Collier Jones

A The Wooden Mile
B The Lighthouse
C The Old Pirate Wreck
D Candlestick Hall
E The Watchtowers
F The Church
G The Village Square
H The Sweet Tooth
I The Grinning Rat

Crampton Rock

Admiral Buggles

The Warning

Stanley Buggles was standing in the drawing room of Candlestick Hall, taking a break and looking up at the portrait of his great-uncle, Admiral Swift. He wished he could tell him all that had happened since he'd inherited the old place from him. Stanley would tell him how he had finally gotten his hands on the ancient silver casket, and that it contained the six candles the Admiral himself had searched for. Right now the six candles were in a pan heating in the kitchen, melting down so that Stanley could retrieve what he thought might lay hidden inside.

Outside the Hall, the wind had picked up. The grass blew in circles around the lawn, the sun shone through the windows, and the breeze sent the flower tops dancing here and there.

Crack, crack, came an unfamiliar noise that drew Stanley to the window. A carrion crow was standing on the ledge, pecking at the glass.

Stanley went right up to it but it wasn't afraid. The crow was going berserk, flapping and beating its dark wings and staring right at him. *Crack, crack*, it continued.

"Shoo, shoo," said Stanley. "Go on!" He banged back on the pane until it took off. This was not like Stanley—he was a great bird lover, and normally he would have stared at it all day, what with it so close, but it had spooked him.

"Do you have a minute, lad?" came Victor's voice, distracting Stanley from his thoughts.

Victor had settled in well since his return to the island a few weeks before. Both he and Mrs. Carelli, his wife, made good housekeepers. He did the gardens and repair work. She did the cooking and cleaning. Stanley did . . . well, not much, but then again the place did belong to him. He wasn't lazy, he was just busy doing nothing, he would joke—and then he would be off on some adventure through the house.

Things had changed for Stanley recently: he was going to make a permanent home on Crampton Rock. He had decided, along with his mother, that he would live there under the supervision of Mr. and Mrs. Carelli. And yes, his mother would visit from time to time, but mostly he would be out here on the Rock alone with them—and so far, he was loving every minute.

"How about that, lad? Is that how you wanted it?" asked Victor. He was pointing to the pike on the wall. He was in a spanking new, freshly polished glass case—just like his old one, but better. And he was back in his favorite spot, under the staircase.

"Excellent," said Stanley. "Thank you,

Victor. He will be delighted, I'm sure."

As they walked away, the pike was already mumbling to himself.

"About time too," he grumbled. "I couldn't have stayed in that old cupboard a moment longer. I have had quite enough of wild adventures and being hurled around from one place to another. I should be quite happy to remain here for now, thank you very much."

Finally, the pike settled into a long sleep. But as he slept, something disturbed him. He dreamed that a black cloud settled over

the house, and that darkness was about to
descend in some strange form.

☠

Victor had turned to outside duties and
Stanley was alone in the kitchen. He stood
over the stove and waited impatiently as the
wax turned to a clear liquid. And as it did, six
pieces of parchment were revealed. Each was
curled up from its long sleep hidden inside
the candles.

Stanley picked them out of the pan and
laid them out on to the table. When all of the
papers had cooled down, he fiddled around
with them, flattening the pieces and fitting
together the jigsaw puzzle of pages.

Once he had put the pieces together, he
could see that they held a complex set of
instructions. But there was a large hole in
the middle of the puzzle! It was almost as if a

diagram had been scissored out of the center, with indications scribbled around it pointing this way and that. Why was the map not complete? It made no sense.

Just as Stanley was mulling over this dilemma, Victor returned.

"I'm sorry to bother you again, lad, but you must come outside and take a look at this."

"At what?" asked Stanley. But Victor was already out the door.

Stanley gathered the pieces of his map and on his way through the hallway placed them carefully into a drawer. He would put them in his room later. The door was open and Stanley walked outside to find Victor standing on the long pathway, staring upward.

What looked like a thousand black crows had descended onto the roof of Candlestick Hall, squawking and flapping and making a terrible racket. There were so many they seemed to darken the sky.

Stanley had often seen the birds perched on a building in the village, but now they had

claimed the top of
his house as their own.
What had brought
them there?

Victor and Stanley were joined by Mrs.
Carelli, returning from the village. She was
armed with bags of this and that, and stood
craning her neck up at the black veil that
covered the tiles.

"What on earth is that all about?" she
called.

"Perhaps it *means* something," said Stanley.
He knew enough about carrion crows not
to trust them. Looking like funeral guests in

their dark hoods and sooty black coats, they were the craftiest of egg thieves and would think nothing of preying on young chicks.

Before Stanley and Victor could turn inside, one of the crows abruptly swooped down and took a fierce peck at Stanley. It clawed at him and its feet got stuck in his long hair.

Mrs. Carelli batted it off. "Shoo, shoo!" Victor swung his rake in the air as the bird persisted in attacking Stanley. The three of them fumbled their way toward the doorway, but the bird hung on still. In a panic, Stanley closed his hands around its body and hurled it back into the air as they ran inside.

Safe indoors, disheveled and shaken, they turned to one another and laughed. Pulling themselves together, they looked out through the window that took in the view of the harbor. Some crows had landed on the front lawn, and one was at the window again, pecking.

Stanley's face grew serious. He watched for a while, until the birds returned to the roof.

"I've never seen no such birds attacking anyone, Victor," Mrs. Carelli insisted, looking at him for an explanation.

Victor shrugged his shoulders. "Must be something in the breeze."

But Stanley had a feeling that more than the weather had changed the mood of these sinister creatures. He took the pieces of map and went upstairs, where he pored over the details again, distracting himself from his thoughts of the baleful black birds.

The Darklings

Out on the moor, the gypsies were busying themselves with daily life. They had recently returned to the island after a long spell away and were perched in place among the hills. The children played in noisy groups, and the men were out gathering firewood or mending wagon wheels.

Greta was the wise old woman of the

camp, the one they all turned to for help and advice. Right now, she was sitting at the table gazing uneasily into her glass ball. Smoke had clouded the vision in the glass, but now it cleared. A face, no, two faces. A man, and then a woman who walked behind him. But they were not alone. Three children trailed behind the woman in a straight line. They were parading through the village, then heading past the harbor, turning up toward Candlestick Hall.

And then the vision clouded over and it was lost.

"Aah, curses," said Greta. "Some foul deed tries to show itself in the glass, but the mist is thick and I cannot see. What is it this time? Someone seeks to darken Stanley's door, and for no good reason." She sighed in frustration, covered the glass ball with its velvet cloth, and walked outside to take in the fresh air.

Back at the Hall, Stanley was showing the map to his close ally, Daisy Grouse. "Look, Daisy. The map's quite clear, but there's a great gaping hole in the middle."

There was no fooling Daisy; she had a good head on her shoulders. The pair of them made a good team and they were as thick as thieves. When Daisy wasn't at her uncle's home in the lighthouse, you could be sure she was here at the Hall.

"Let me try," she insisted. She attempted to put the pieces together differently but no, Stanley was right. It looked as if someone had torn a neat shape from its middle.

"What about our good friend the pike?" suggested Daisy. "Does he know we have the map? Surely he can tell us something."

"Maybe," said Stanley. "He's been busy settling into his new home, but he should be back to normal by now, I would think." They gathered up the pieces and ran downstairs.

Stanley knew only too well that the pike would speak if he felt the need to, but that he was not always in a talkative mood.

"We thought perhaps you might have an opinion on our map here!" said Stanley gingerly. "There appears to be something missing from the middle. Does that mean anything to you at all?"

"I fear you have a far more pressing matter to attend to, my dear boy, and I would give it my fullest attention if you wish to remain at the Hall."

Stanley stared at him in frustration, but that was all the pike would say.

BANG, BANG, BANG.

Someone was rapping heavily at the door. Daisy grabbed the map and sneaked it into a nearby drawer.

Mrs. Carelli was coming down the staircase and all three of them got to the front door together.

Mrs. Carelli opened the door. "Ahhh . . . err . . . Mister . . . and Mrs. . . . Darkling, isn't it?" she said. Stanley noticed that her voice seemed shaky.

Looking back at them was the strangest-looking group of people Stanley and Daisy had ever seen.

"My name is Edmund Darkling, and this is my wife, Grace," explained the man standing in the doorway. He wore no expression, and his manner was cold and unnerving. "This is our eldest daughter, Annabelle, and these are our twins, Olive and Berkeley."

A long streak of a girl and an identical-looking pair of younger children glared back at them. The younger girl carried a headless doll, and her twin had his hands behind his back and a look on his face that swore he was up to no good. They were dressed in deeply somber-colored clothes with frilled sleeves and collars. All wore knitted brows and sullen mouths.

Stanley studied their faces. There was something shocking in their appearance, something unusual about their features, but he couldn't quite decide what it was. Their eyebrows were thick and black and maddened their eyes. Their hair was straight and thin.

Mr. Darkling had paused before speaking

again and Stanley felt as if he should say something, but it wouldn't come. He longed to shut the door on them, but his good manners betrayed him. He shifted nervously.

Right then, one of the crows descended from the roof, landed on Mr. Darkling's hat, and hopped down to rest peacefully on his shoulder.

"I have good reason to darken your door, Stanley," he announced, staring directly at Stanley. "Now listen carefully. I wish to inform you that, as the true and rightful owner of the Darkling residence, the one you now stand in and refer to as Candlestick Hall, I wish to return with my family so that we may resume our position here. There is much to do and we need you to vacate the premises within seven days."

He said it almost as if what he said had no

consequence for them. There was no emotion in his voice, no regret or embarrassment at the circumstances.

Stanley quickly made sense of what had just been said to him. The man now standing at his door was claiming to be the rightful owner of Candlestick Hall.

But Mrs. Carelli's nervousness had left her, and now her blood was boiling at the thought that these people could just walk up to the door and absurdly lay claim to the house.

"Young Stanley Buggles here is the rightful owner of Candlestick Hall. He inherited it from his great-uncle, Admiral Swift. I am his housekeeper and I would thank you kindly, sir, if you would clear off our land," she thundered. She tried to shut the door, but the Darkling boy had stepped quickly inside the frame, and she stopped short of crushing his foot.

"Aah yes, Admiral Swift," continued Mr. Darkling, his expression still unmoved. "The pirate who terrorized the Darklings and forced us to give up the house when I was a mere boy. It is hard to believe that the pleasant-looking young man in front of me is descended from a line of villainous piracy. Now, will you please ensure that our things are left behind when you go? I would not wish to find a ransacked house on my arrival. We shall be here in a week. Unless, of course, you can prove your claim to this place." An evil smile lifted the corner of his mouth.

The crow flew from his shoulder as all five of them turned and left. As they marched down the pathway, the twins turned at the same time and stuck out their pointed tongues at Stanley.

In shock, Daisy and Mrs. Carelli retreated to make a hot drink, while Stanley wandered around the house. He took a good long look at all the weird and wonderful things that filled the Hall from top to bottom. Animal heads in jars, skulls and skeletons, stuffed wildlife caught in traps and snares. He chewed over his thoughts of the unusual family that had stood at his door.

Were all these things really *theirs*?

Were they really the rightful owners of Candlestick Hall? And would he soon be homeless on the island he had grown to love so much?

3

The Loophole

"First things first. Forget the map for now," said Daisy, as she returned it to Stanley's room and placed it back in the silver casket. She was the only one apart from Stanley who knew of the casket's home behind the false panel in the cupboard.

Next, they all sat around the kitchen table and got the papers out. Deeds, death certificates, other documents that Stanley knew would make sense to somebody, but not to him.

"Victor, it was you yourself who recently told me that the old place used to be named Darkling Hall," piped up Stanley.

"That's true, Stanley. But the Darklings have lived in the village for many years now. Your Great-uncle Bart bought Darkling Hall in good faith, I'm sure. We need to go through all this with a fine-tooth comb, lad."

Victor looked over everything meticulously. He read everything from back to front, inside out and back again, peering over his glasses and making little notes to himself on a long sheet of paper.

Mrs. Carelli was busying herself. "I'll deal wi' getting back to normality," she said, as she cranked up the wood burner in the kitchen and rolled out pastry, grumbling to herself about how the Darklings were a disgrace to common decency.

☠

Stanley and Daisy decided that they needed advice from the Mayoress of the Rock, so they headed into the village. But as soon as they left the Hall, a crow appeared and danced around their feet, almost as if to stop them from going anywhere. It didn't seem at all perturbed by their presence.

Two more birds appeared, their eyes glowing like little moons. Then abruptly there were five or six, clawing and pecking at Stanley's head. Daisy waved them off with her hands, and they scratched at her with black talons.

They ran down to the village and could escape only by heading into the village hall, heaving the door closed behind them.

The Mayoress, Penelope Spoonbill, was standing there waiting, almost as if she had expected them. She was a slight woman, with her hair pulled back and a beak of a nose. Her hands were clasped together. There was something fragile about her spindly form, but she had an air of authority about her.

"Good morning, Stanley. You seem a little flustered, but I see you have had the good sense to bring help and support. You may need it."

"Why do you say that?" asked Stanley.

"I'm afraid our friend Mister Darkling is ahead of you, Stanley. He has already sought my advice, and he insists that Darkling Hall was taken from his family many years ago, when I myself was only a young girl. I recall nothing of his claim."

"But why *now*?" asked Stanley.

"I think the Darklings feared your great-uncle, Stanley. And when you first came here you were beset with troubles of one kind and another. But you have solved many problems now for the Hall, and she sits in peace at last. You have done the work for them, and the time was right for them to make their move," she suggested.

"But his claim is ridiculous," said Stanley, "and no one would ever take it seriously. Surely the strict laws of Crampton Rock will protect us?"

"Of course, Stanley. No one has the right just to declare that something belongs to them, without foundation to their claim. It is up to them to prove their assertion, not you. I trust you have your deeds?" the Mayoress asked.

"Yes, of course," Stanley said.

Penelope Spoonbill took out a large book entitled *Property Law*. "Let's take a look," she said. "You should be warned, though, that Mister Darkling has seen these details already. He must feel he has something to hold over you."

She opened the book at a marked page and ran a long finger down the paragraphs. Then she stopped and tracked back to the beginning of a long sentence. "Here it is," she said.

> *Where a dispute of ownership is contested, the presentation of property deeds shall establish the rightful owner unless proof to the contrary can be determined by evidence written in stone.*

"What does that mean, in plain speaking?" asked Daisy.

"Well, what it means," began Miss Spoonbill, "is that if Stanley has the deeds and they show his name as being the owner of the Candlestick estate, then he is fine."

"And what about the last bit?" asked Stanley. "Something about 'written in stone'?"

"Oh, don't worry about that, Stanley. It means that if somewhere it was written in stone that the Darklings owned the house, there would be an argument for their case. It's really an old way of saying, 'unless the impossible should happen,' that's all. These old documents are worded funnily sometimes."

But worry about it Stanley did. And even before he reached home again, his fears had begun to trouble him.

The light was dropping as they left the village hall, and the Darkling twins were hanging around outside the door. They stared at Stanley as he and Daisy left the building.

"Hello, Stanley. Who's that?" Olive asked, cradling her headless doll in her arms.

"Err . . . hello, Olive," replied Stanley. "This is my friend Daisy."

"Isn't she pretty!" she said, and then both she and Berkeley ran away screaming and laughing into the darkness of the streets.

"I'm afraid they're . . . well, a little bit . . . odd," muttered Stanley, almost feeling as if he had to apologize to Daisy on their behalf.

The fire baskets were burning in the harbor to guide the ships safely into port, and the lights in the windows at the hall lit the short trail back home.

But there was something going on outside the door of the Hall. A small group of people, three or four maybe, one of them holding a light, stood there. A faint *clink, clink, clink* resounded across the street.

Stanley noticed that the crows were still and silent on the roof. "It must be the Darklings," he insisted. "Otherwise those birds would be going mad."

Sure enough, Edmund Darkling was holding a lamp up to the pillar at the right-hand side of the front door. Another man was chipping at the cement work with small masonry tools. Mr. and Mrs. Carelli were standing there too, looking most displeased.

"You have no right to be here," complained Mrs. Carelli. "It's an outrage!"

"What's going on?" asked Stanley.

"Patience, please," said Mr. Darkling in his calm, deep tone. "I do believe we are about to retrieve a result."

The stonemason pulled at the now-loose brickwork, and out came a large block. He turned it around, and from its previously hidden side he rubbed away years of dust and dirt to reveal a word, written in stone.

The Darkling Curse

"I'm sorry," said Miss Spoonbill. "I am not above the law. I see your problem, yet I feel there is nothing I can do.'"

She was sitting in Candlestick Hall with Stanley and the Carellis, explaining the current situation. Now that "proof in stone" had been revealed, the Darkling family had a claim on the house. This meant that it was

41

now possible that Candlestick Hall could be put back in their hands.

"Until the case is settled in the court, the

Darkling family is allowed to reside in the house. That is the law of the Rock."

And no sooner had she left than the Darklings were arriving. Between them, they pulled and pushed a long open-backed cart up the path, filled with odd things. A coffin and several long coats, cloaks, and tall hats. Macabre paintings of their grim-looking ancestors. Heaps of morbid-looking decorations. Strangely shaped jars and medicine bottles. Boxes of dusty, handwritten books dribbled with candle wax. Long black velvet curtains.

Much of it, Stanley noticed, was like the things already in the house.

A stack of wooden boxes marked "fragile" and "do not touch" filled one end of the cart, with strange hisses and rattles coming from them.

"What on earth have you got in there?" asked Mrs. Carelli. "You can't just bring anything here, you know."

"These things are my personal and private possessions, Mrs. Carelli. So please, do your job and help me bring them inside." said Mr. Darkling.

"I don't work for the Darklings. I work for

the lad. 'Tis he that pays me, not you. So, no, I won't be helping you," she told him, storming off inside.

An uncomfortable commotion followed. Stanley insisted that the living quarters in the house be divided and that he should keep the side where his bedroom was. The Darklings were adamant that they should be allowed access to the whole house. But Stanley was backed up by Mrs. Carelli and Victor.

"May I remind you, sir, that you haven't proven anything yet," insisted Stanley as he turned to Mr. Darkling. He found it hard to stand up to him, but he was forcing himself to do it. "And as far as I am concerned, we have been more than accommodating already. So if you don't mind, that will be the agreement under which you are given the key to the house. Thank you for your cooperation."

Stanley turned and walked away, a grin breaking across his face. Mr. Darkling's eyes narrowed as he stared at Stanley. Then he paced off noisily in the direction of *his* side of the house.

"Well done, lad. You stuck to your guns. You did right," said Victor.

Stanley ran up the stairs and for the first time ever he locked his bedroom door. Then he left, to seek solace with his friends out on the moor.

He left the house through the back door and escaped over the garden gate. But the crows spotted him, and once more he was forced to beat off their attack with flailing hands and arms.

When he reached the hills, the cawing and crying of the birds petered away, and his mood lifted as he made out the faces of his friends. Big Bartley was chopping wood and wiping the sweat from his brow. The children were running around in circles and making the dogs bark. His good friend Phinn was feeding a hawk that sat perched on his gloved arm. Stanley spent the next ten minutes watching the hawk from close up as it feasted on the remains of a rabbit.

Greta's head popped out from inside her

wagon, and she called him over. The younger children were fussing around Stanley, pulling at his shirt, eager for him to play, but she sent them away and Stanley could see that something was bothering her.

"Come inside, lad," she beckoned. "I have much to tell you."

The roof of her small wagon was curved and shaped from old timber. Bits of heather hung from the ceiling, and pots and pans, all beautifully painted, were scattered about. A table and seats took up the space at the far end, and they sat down together.

"The glass ball has been hard at work, Stanley," Greta began. "I already know your predicament. It is some time since I set eyes upon the Darklings, but I am only too familiar with their bloodline. Now listen carefully.

"Many years ago, a keen businessman

came to live on the Rock, and paid the locals to build a house for him. But to his great misfortune, he suffered an attack from the werewolf while returning home late one night. He survived, but he had been bitten, and fell under the werewolf's curse. And when he foolishly fathered a family, the blood of the beast ran through his veins and into those of his children.

"He was a good man, but eventually the curse overtook him, and his animal antics became too much for his weakening body. In the end, it destroyed him. He left behind a widow and three boys. The strains of the beast showed in his offspring and eventually in their own children too. They were not werewolves, but their habits were almost doglike. They ate raw meat and stalked the streets in a pack at night. They slept in the

Brice Darkling

day and kept the whole village awake in the late hours with strange calls and howls."

"And who was this man, the forefather to these people?" asked Stanley.

"His name was Brice Darkling," she

announced. "And what became known as the Darkling Curse was familiar to the people here for many years."

"And the house that Brice Darkling built for his family?" he questioned.

"Darkling Hall, Stanley."

"I thought as much."

"Edmund Darkling is a distant relative of Brice. His family still bears the lupine traces. He lived at the Hall until he was about your age," explained Greta.

They were interrupted as Bartley appeared in the open carriage doorway. Bartley was a huge man with a big heart, warm and friendly but fierce and fearless when the need arose. He held out a large hand to shake Stanley's.

"I don't know how you do it, Stanley. Either trouble follows you, or *you* follow *it*. It looks like we have another fight on our hands, although this time it looks like our boxing skills will be of no use."

"There will be a way," said Greta. "There is always a way."

Stanley's mood had dropped again by the time he returned to the Hall. He knew that he would have to battle with the birds before he even got through the door. That was bad enough, but now he had no idea what he might find inside. In the past, he had sought refuge from all his troubles in the house. But now his problems held him hostage inside his own walls.

Back inside, he straightened his ruffled hair and nursed the scratches on his hands made by the crows. The house was silent. Too silent. There were five more people living here now. Where were they, and what were they doing?

He walked down the dark corridor to his room thinking troubled thoughts. As he placed the key in the lock, a breathing noise sounded behind him. Somehow, he couldn't turn around. He froze, hoping that he had imagined it, but no—if anything, it was getting louder.

Stanley forced himself to turn and look. At the far end of the corridor, the still and brooding shape of a black dog stared back at him. Where on earth had it come from? It was huge, long and lanky with its head held low, its eyes fixed on him.

Carefully, Stanley turned the key. And then swiftly he tugged at the door and shot inside—but he tripped on the rug and went sprawling across the wooden floor. Four legs thundered down the bare boards of the corridor, and Stanley lay helpless as the hound raced around the door. It rushed toward him and stood snarling over him, saliva dripping from its open jaws. Stanley shut his eyes tight. He couldn't bear to watch.

"Steadman!" came a young voice. "*Stead-man.* Come here, boy."

The dog obediently turned and trotted innocently up to Berkeley, who stood in the doorway alone.

"He only wants to play," grinned Berkeley.

Stanley was too shocked to say anything. He simply got to his feet and pushed his door shut, locking it on the inside and wiping the sweat from his brow.

That night he barely slept and he wasn't sure if it was out of fear or because the incessant noise in the house kept him awake.

Over the next few days he noticed a pattern emerging.

Through the hours of sunlight, the Darklings were still and silent and confined to their rooms. But as the night drew in, they would grow noisy, emerging from their sleep.

5
Wonderful Daisy

It was the end of another day. As Stanley sat on his bed, something down at the harbor caught his eye: flickering candlelight in Daisy's bedroom window over at the lighthouse. To anyone else it was just a light, but to Stanley it meant that Daisy was contacting him. Either she had information that would help, or she needed him. She signaled one more time to say that she would come over in the morning.

The next day Stanley was outside, ready to beat off the crows, when Daisy came. He held a long garden rake and swished it around as they swooped down on the pathway.

Daisy ran through the falling black feathers and they raced inside. As they slammed the door shut, Mr. and Mrs. Darkling emerged into the hallway. "It is not in the interests of the Rock to be attacking the crow population, Stanley," began Mr. Darkling. Steadman was lurking behind him, making Daisy and Stanley nervous. A low grumble emitted from the dog's belly.

"You brought those birds here," came a voice from the kitchen. It was Mrs. Carelli. She was covered in flour and pointing a spoon toward him like a sword. "It isn't the lad's fault he has to protect himself and his visitors. Come on, you two," she said. "We have fresh bread in the oven."

☠

Later, the two friends went up to Stanley's room. At the top of the staircase, Steadman was guarding the doors on the Darkling side of the landing. He got to his feet as they reached the top step and growled at them as they tiptoed by, petrified.

As they turned into Stanley's room, Olive and Berkeley appeared right behind them.

"Arghh!" cried Stanley. "I wish you wouldn't do that!"

"Do you want to play with us?" they asked, speaking in unison.

"Er . . . no. I'm sorry, we're . . . busy. There is something important we have to do."

They were saved by Mr. Darkling. "Children. Go to your rooms at once."

Stanley and Daisy scrambled into Stanley's room before Mr. Darkling could say anything to them.

In the safety of Stanley's room, behind the locked door, Daisy could finally work on her idea.

Across the surfaces of his bedroom furniture all kinds of papers were laid out: the deeds to the Hall, plans of the house, and a map of the island. Daisy pored over the details. She asked Stanley to take out the silver casket and assemble the map pieces again.

"Mmmm. Exactly as I thought!" she said jubilantly.

"What?" said Stanley. He was on pins, waiting for her to explain.

She laid out the map of the island next to the map from the silver casket.

"Now do

you see it?" she asked, grinning wildly.

"No!" he answered. He was getting frustrated.

"The hole in the middle of the map, Stanley. It's not a hole at all. Don't you see? It's exactly the same shape as Crampton Rock."

Stanley examined it more closely. She was right! What at first had appeared to be a piece torn out of the middle of the map was in fact a carefully crafted hole the same shape as the island.

After all this time! Discovering the silver casket and revealing the maps inside the candles had been a journey in itself, but to discover that this map might lead to something else sent an excited shiver down Stanley's spine. Where did the map lead? What would it reveal? Could they keep it a secret? All these thoughts buzzed around inside his head.

They looked at the instructions again, starting from the top. Stanley mumbled out loud to himself, trying to make sense of what he read. But soon he realized that there might be a problem.

"Daisy, we can't do this yet!"

"Why not?"

"Well, what if we find out where the map leads and we discover something . . . You know, something special and valuable. What would we do with it? My possessions are already in jeopardy. If I kept something here in this house I might end up losing it, along with everything else. I am already worried about losing the silver casket. Those Darkling children are little snoops, and they're already spending half their time spying on us. We should deal with the Darklings before we explore the map."

"You're right," Daisy admitted. "We need

to bide our time until this crazy nonsense is over with."

They put everything neatly away, in the hope that soon they would be able to return to the treasure hunt.

For the time being, Stanley was keen for Daisy to join him in a small adventure. He explained to her that he had grown concerned at how quiet the Darklings were in the day. As the sun shone down on the Rock, their curtains stayed closed and their silence was unnerving. But at night they became active, and strange noises echoed down the corridors.

"One night, Mrs. Carelli left her bed to see what was going on and she was so disturbed by what she saw that she fled to her room and locked the door," he explained.

"And . . . what was it?" quizzed Daisy.

"I don't know," he admitted. "She still won't

tell me! You must join me, Daisy," begged Stanley. "I need to see what they are up to. Will you come with me to the Darkling side of the house?"

Daisy agreed, but Stanley could see that she was not keen on his idea. Neither was he. It was just something that had to be done.

Through all the excitement, a moment's distraction meant that Stanley had, unintentionally, let his guard down. As he and Daisy left his room to head for the kitchen, he left the door to his room unlocked.

Who killed poor Stanley?

The two heroes sat in the kitchen scullery, whispering about their route through the secret panels of the house as they devoured Mrs. Carelli's newly baked bread and gulped half a jug of fresh milk.

Within ten minutes they were crawling through the secret passageways that ran inside the walls of the building. Stanley had discovered some of these in the past, but Daisy showed him that there were many more.

They made their way to the Darkling side still covered in crumbs and milk stains, giggling quietly as they sneaked along in the dark.

Daisy led the way. "Quiet," she whispered. "We're close now." It was likely that she knew the house better than anyone. Much of what she knew wasn't even in the original plans of the house. Stanley wondered what Brice Darkling had had in mind when he built these secret routes, all those years ago.

Soon they were alongside the Darkling quarters, and Daisy peeked in through a wrought-iron grating. She could just make out the shape of Mr. Darkling lying asleep on the bed.

Stanley squashed up alongside Daisy, and they watched Mr. Darkling's upper body gently rise and fall. But it was not what Stanley would have called sleep, not a curled-up, warm, enveloped snooze. No. Mr. Darkling lay with his hands crossed across his chest in a cold, mournful doze that looked more like a short slice of death. He was still dressed in his sinister black outfit and looked as if he should be staring out from an open coffin.

Daisy and Stanley peered around the room. Several glass tanks were scattered around, but they couldn't see what was in them. The room was clean and tidy but had a strange smell.

Steadman rose up from the floor, taking them by surprise. He rushed over to the vent, sniffing noisily and baring his teeth at them.

Mr. Darkling woke with a start. "What is it, old boy?" he asked, and his face appeared up close, inspecting the grate.

Stanley and Daisy ducked their heads and hid in the darkness of the corridor. If Mr. Darkling had explored the house as much as Stanley when he was a boy, he would know the way into the passage.

Mrs. Darkling walked into the bedroom. "What is it, Edmund?"

"I'm not sure, dear, but I think perhaps we have visitors. Mice or rats maybe. Or possibly something bigger!" He rubbed his chin in thought.

By this time Steadman was going crazy, snapping and snarling, and he woke Annabelle and Olive in the next room. Stanley and Daisy had now slid long out of harm's way and were alongside the girls' room. They pressed their faces up to the next grating. The girls were sitting up in bed, clapping their hands together in sequence and reciting a strange verse that sent a chill from Stanley's head to his toes.

> "Who killed poor Stanley?" "I," said the
>   Crow,
> "With a shot from my bow, I killed poor
>   Stanley."
> "Who caught his blood?" "I," said the Fish,
> "With my little dish, I caught his blood."
> "Who'll make the shroud ..."

"Girls, please. You are making too much noise," said Mrs. Darkling, poking her head around the door. "We are trying to sleep. You should be doing the same."

Behind Stanley and Daisy, the familiar sound of panting was coming down the narrow passage. It was Steadman—Mr. Darkling must have sent him to investigate. They scrambled away in a fast crawl as the noise of his breathing came closer. In desperation, Daisy pushed the grating out into the next room along the passageway, and they burst through the hole, pulling the cover back over as they went. Fortunately, the room was empty, the covers pulled back on the bed.

It was Berkeley's room, but he was nowhere to be seen.

A strange smell filled the air. Sinister-looking wooden toys were spilled across the floor, and handprints and scribbles covered the walls. What a mess!

What seemed like hundreds of little bottles, filled with liquids of all manner of different colors, were stacked along the top of a chest of drawers. Some of them bubbled away, and in one there was a cloudy effervescence that looked as if it might burst the bottle open at any second.

The sound of feet echoed from the

landing. Daisy dived under the bed, and Stanley instinctively jumped for cover under the sheets, pulling them right over his head. Only a fraction of a second later, Mr. Darkling appeared around the door.

"At least someone has remained un- d i s t u r b e d ," he said as he glanced at the lump in the bed.

Steadman was now snarling and sniffing through the grating in Berkeley's room.

"Back to your bed, old boy," instructed Mr. Darkling as he closed the door and left.

"That was close," said Daisy as her face peered out from under the bed. "Let's get out of here before Berkeley returns."

When they were sure that Steadman had cleared out of the secret passageway, they lifted the grating and climbed back in, taking a longer route to avoid going back the way they had come.

The verse that the girls had recited was ringing in Stanley's head.

They were now descending a narrow staircase to the ground floor. Daisy remembered the little doorway that opened up onto the hearth of the scullery, right back where they had started. Finally, Stanley peered out through the stony cold of the fireplace.

"Yep, it's clear," he said, jumping down.

Covered in soot, they sat back down in their chairs and drank the last of the jug of milk.

But all the while they had been searching on the Darkling side of the house, someone else had had a similar idea. Someone who only Stanley and Daisy knew was missing from his bed. And as they scraped the bread-crumbs from their plates with sooty black fingers and drank the last drops from the milk jug, young Berkeley was creeping across the hallway back to his room, with his hands full.

7

The Old Candle Shop.

At breakfast, Victor was explaining his plans to Stanley and Mrs. Carelli as they sat at the kitchen table.

"I cannot attend to the garden here," he admitted. "Every time I step outside the door the birds attack. It is the same for all of us. So I have decided to spend some time cleaning out the candle shop. If they throw us out of here we have no home and no work, and the old shop may have to become our refuge. Stanley, if that happens, you will come with me and Violet. I will make room for all of us."

"You're very kind," said Stanley.

"Not at all," said Victor. "I owe you everything I have. It was you who saved me when I sat marooned out on Scarecrow Point. Now I may have to save *you*."

"In that case, I shall come and help you," Stanley declared.

"Well in all my days I've never heard anything like it," began Mrs. Carelli. "Here he is, lord of the manor, sat in his mansion and never lifted a finger since the day he arrived. But show him a bruised and battered old candle shop and he's armed with brooms and brushes and off like a shot."

They all laughed out loud and for a brief moment Stanley remembered the time before the Darklings arrived and how happy they'd been. Would it ever be the same again?

They packed Victor's work tools and put them into a small

cart. Mrs. Carelli made a large picnic bundle and placed it in Stanley's arms. Then they set off, attempting to beat off the birds as they went.

Soon they were down in the village, passing through the square and the hustle and bustle of life, past the old sweet shop and the village hall. Outside the old candle shop on the corner they stopped and entered. For the first time in many years the key was turned inside the rusty lock. Cobwebs clung hard as if to hold the door shut. A damp smell hit them immediately, and Victor pushed the windows open.

He puttered around, checking through boxes of candles and looking here and there for this and that while Stanley also investigated. The shop was at the front, and behind the counter was access to the back rooms, and a back door leading out to the beehives where the wax was collected for the candles. Beyond that was the way onto the moor.

One of the back rooms was larger than Stanley expected, a huge space where all the candles had been made. There was a big vat like a bath in the middle of the floor, with worktop space around it. Candles hung on lengths of wick, suspended from ropes that ran from one end of the room to the other.

Upstairs, there were three smaller rooms: one with a tin bath and a large jug in it, the others with beds. Everything was caked in dust.

Soon they were hard at work, scrubbing the worktops and sweeping the floors. Victor stopped work for a minute to laugh at young Stanley working so hard—Mrs. Carelli would have dropped to the floor to see it, he chuckled.

A little while later, Daisy rapped on one of the windows with a spare brush she held. She let herself in and they spent the rest of the day sprucing up the whole place, dusting, washing, scrubbing.

Mrs. Carelli stayed on at the old Hall. They

knew only too well that if they all left the house, even for just a short time, they would more than likely get locked out for good.

Daisy was busy washing the windows when she caught sight of something familiar out of the corner of her eye. "Stanley, look!"

He moved to the window. It was Berkeley, leaving a rundown old building across the way.

They were watching him with interest when Victor came to their side. "I'm sorry, I neglected to tell you about that. The place opposite, it's the old Darkling place. Hopefully, they'll be returning there soon. Strangely enough, they used to be good customers here," he continued. "It is rumored they spend most of their waking hours in the dark, and they've bought many candles here in the past."

Stanley stared at the house opposite. It

was ramshackle
and shoddy, with
decaying, rotten
timbers and shutters
fastened crookedly
across the windows. A
brick chimney leaned off
a rickety roof. Stanley
remembered that this
was the place where
he had seen the crows
resting before the
Darklings had come to
Candlestick Hall.

8

Something is Missing

When Stanley and Victor returned to the house that evening, something had changed. The birds were perched on the far side of the roof, and there was no swooping or clawing or diving down at their faces. Nothing.

Stanley was puzzled, until he caught sight of someone standing at the foot of the pathway. It was Phinn, holding his hawk on his arm. Every few minutes he released her, and she soared up into the air, circling over the house.

"Greta sent me," he said, as they walked toward him. "She said that soon you would return to the house and that I was to make sure the crows were kept at bay."

Stanley watched the great hawk as she returned and landed on Phinn's outstretched arm. Though she was large and powerful, she was very graceful. She tilted her head and looked at them.

"She's beautiful," said Stanley. He held out his hand gently and stroked the plumage on the underside of her belly.

"Careful, lad. She must like you. She'd normally take a chunk out o' something that came that close."

Stanley knew how to win the confidence

of animals; it was something that came naturally to him. And he felt safe with the crows tucked away on the roof, even when he turned and caught Edmund Darkling peering out from behind a curtain. He enjoyed their brief moment of victory over the Darklings, and remembered what Greta had said to him. "There is always a way."

But as they stepped into the house, Stanley's mood sank. The Darkling children were playing in the hallway, and Mr. Darkling was hanging a portrait on the wall in the dim candlelight. Steadman instantly pinned Stanley and Victor to the door.

"Mister Darkling, we can't be having the dog threatening us every time we walk in. It isn't fair," said Victor. "He should be confined to Darkling quarters." The dog grumbled and stared at him as if he understood every word.

"Get down, Steadman," said Mrs. Darkling, emerging swiftly and disappearing just as quickly, taking Steadman and dragging him awkwardly by his huge collar. She was such a small woman it was hard to imagine how she could muster up the strength.

"Mister Carelli, may I remind you that you are staff here," said Mr. Darkling. "What's more, the hallway is a communal area, since it serves to allow access in and out of the building. Steadman is showing signs of uneasiness in your presence. Perhaps he feels you are a threat to him."

"And on another small matter," continued Victor, ignoring him, "you cannot make changes to the house while the owner-ship is in dispute. The documents clearly state this, so I'm afraid you'll have to take the picture of the little dog down from the wall."

"It is not a little dog, Mister Carelli. It is a picture of my son Berkeley," Mr. Darkling said, red-faced.

"Oh. Begging your pardon, sir," added Victor. "I do apologize. I haven't got my glasses on."

The residents dispersed with embarrassment, and a spell of silence reigned for a short time. But the dark had returned and Stanley knew the Darklings would be up to no good. He had come to realize that if there was a time to watch them, it was at night.

He sat up late in the scullery, tucked in front of the fire, reflecting on the day. When Victor had made his comment on Berkeley's portrait, Stanley had tried to hide his amusement, but he now chuckled quietly to himself as he remembered it.

He drifted into sleep, only to be woken by a tapping in the darkness of the hallway. A voice accompanied it, too faint to be heard.

Stanley slowly raised himself up from his seat and edged his way to look through the crack of the doorway. He couldn't see anything. He tiptoed into the hallway and followed the sound until it took him to the back of the staircase.

And there were Berkeley and Olive. Berkeley was holding a short stick and tapping on the pike's glass case.

"He's ugly, isn't he?" said Olive.

"Yes. And he moved, so he must be alive," said Berkeley.

"He can't move. He's dead," insisted Olive.

"He did. He moved. He moved his *eye*. I saw it," claimed Berkeley, tapping harder and faster on the glass.

Stanley felt that he should intervene at this point, but as he stepped out into the moonlit hall the twins set off, chasing each other around the house, running across the floor on all fours.

Well, that explains the banging and clattering all night long, he thought.

"Stanley, I fear you may be losing your grip on the Candlestick estate." Stanley swung around. It was the pike! He hadn't spoken for some time, not since the Darklings had first laid their gloomy shadow across his door.

"I should hate to become a part of the Darkling furniture," continued the pike. "I much prefer the company of your good self and your staff. Victor has made a wonderful job of my new home. What do you intend to do?"

"I don't know!" Stanley whispered. "Not yet. But Greta says there is always a way."

"Ah, the gypsy lady. A wise old owl,

Stanley, I'm sure. Of course there is always a way. But will you find it?"

Just then, Stanley was thrown off course. "Isn't it a little late for you, Stanley?" came a slow voice. Mr. Darkling was standing in the doorway to the lounge, the moonlight picking out his face and his eyes glowing demonically in the darkness.

"I fell asleep in the scullery. I'm going up now," Stanley said, feeling as though he should explain himself. He hurried to climb the stairs.

"Oh, and Stanley," continued the voice behind him.

Stanley forced himself to stop and turn. "Yes?"

"If I catch you or anyone else snooping around in my private quarters, I shall make sure my dog makes a fast meal out of your

bony little frame. Do you understand me?"

"Of course," Stanley said, trying to keep his voice steady. "Why on earth would I want to do that?"

But when he reached his room his fright turned to anger. He had left the door unlocked the night before! Quickly he ran to his cupboard and pulled back the false panel. The space where the silver casket should have sat was empty.

"Oh no. No," he whispered. He searched again, bringing the candle closer. Perhaps he had missed it. But no, it was gone.

"*Berkeley,*" he said to himself in a heavy tone. Berkeley was into everything. Climbing here, searching there, crawling under and over, weaving his way in and out of this and that, knocking things over, breaking the vases that adorned the rooms. He was like an oversized rat scuttling around the place.

Stanley knew there was no point confronting Berkeley. He would only deny it. Instead, under the meager candlelight, he forgot all that had been said and decided to work his way back through the secret corridors.

But first he needed something from the kitchen. He glided down the staircase and slipped into the pantry. Then it was back into the scullery and up through the chimney enclosure.

Even in his rush of anger, he really did not like the idea of entering the Darkling domain in the dead of night. He had escaped discovery the last time only by the skin of his teeth. This time he was alone and the way ahead was pitch black.

As he drew near the Darkling quarters he could hear music, the deep and somber sound of something slow and funereal. As Stanley peered through the grating to Mr. Darkling's room, he could see that it was empty. A light burned in the corner and he could see something moving in the glass tanks, hissing and rattling. Snakes! Real, living, moving snakes.

The darkness up ahead of him suddenly grew more frightening. What if the snakes could move around, slinking about under the floors and in and out of the walls?

Stanley tried to concentrate. Up ahead there were more empty rooms, first the girls' and then Berkeley's. But there was no sign of the children. Where were they? Quietly, he levered open the grating to Berkeley's room and stole inside, taking care with the candle in his hand.

He eased open every drawer. Nothing. There were many places the casket might be; it was small and compact; but he had a feeling Berkeley had not spent much time in his room. Nothing seemed to have been moved since his last visit. Stanley searched harder, listening to the music continuing somewhere nearby. But still, nothing.

Pausing a moment, Stanley realized that the music was coming from the rounded tower that perched on the gable end of the house. He was eager to see what was going on, and he knew he could peer through the ceiling of the tower if he got into the loft. He poked his head around the doorway of Berkeley's room into the dim light of the corridor.

Sensing that no one was there, he made his way across the passageway on tiptoe. He pulled gently at a section of wainscoting, disclosing a cobwebbed doorway that probably only he knew about.

But something had touched his neck. Something cold and damp. Little by little, Stanley turned around. It was Steadman, pinning him to the wall with the point of his nose.

The whites of the dog's eyes were fluorescent in the dark. Stanley sensed the heaviness of a bark welling up inside Steadman's throat. But before it happened, Stanley slid his hand into his pocket and handed the dog a chunk of red meat.

That was all it took. Steadman's head jolted as he threw the meat back into his mouth and ground his teeth into the tasty morsel. Then he slung it greedily down his throat and looked excitedly at Stanley. Another piece came. And then another.

The music continued as Stanley got ready to make his final move. He dangled a final piece at Steadman, patted the dog's head as he caught it, and then disappeared behind the panel. The last piece of meat was still in his pocket. He knew he might need it on the way back.

Steadman stood mesmerized. Where had

his newfound friend gone? The pleasant-looking one with the meat who he had thought was his enemy, but suddenly realized was not so bad after all.

☠

Meanwhile, Stanley had made it into the circular loft area over the tower. The music was closer and louder now. He tried to see down through the boards, but the gaps were tiny and he only caught glimpses here and there. Finally, he found a spot where he could see half of the room.

It was Mrs. Darkling making music at this late hour. She stood with a large double bass, her beady little eyes closed, moving her head gracefully as she played.

Mr. Darkling was there also, standing up and holding something in both hands. It was a large glass bell jar. Stanley had to narrow his eyes to concentrate on what was inside it. It appeared to be a black snake, contained in a liquid, and Stanley was certain it was some mutated form, as it seemed to bear two heads.

Mr. Darkling held up the jar and closed his

eyes. He whispered something through the glass, and Stanley was sure that as he did so the snake shifted slightly in its prison.

He knew that the Darkling children were there also, although he could see only their feet as they sat together on a long cushioned seat.

Mr. Darkling opened the top of the glass jar. Only Stanley's excellent knowledge of the animal kingdom let him recognize what he was seeing. The sleek black form wound its way upward out of the liquid and, as Mr. Darkling watched with a contented expression, it slithered away under the floorboards.

Stanley had seen enough to know what was heading toward his side of the house. It was a Black Crow Snake!

To add to his horror, the girls began to repeat the verse again.

> "Who killed poor Stanley?" "I," said the Crow,
> "With a shot from my bow, I killed poor
>   Stanley."
> "Who caught his blood?" "I," said the Fish,
> "With my little dish, I caught his blood."
> "Who'll make the shroud?" "I," said the Beetle,
> "With my thread and needle, I'll make the
>   shroud."
> "Who'll dig the grave?" "I," said the Owl,
> "With my pick and shovel, I'll dig the grave."
> "And what of the Hall, empty and bare?

Who will take care?"
"We," said the children. "Along with our
    kin, we shall step in.
We will take care."

The music stopped and the verse ended. Stanley sat in shock. He realized that the Darkling plan was far more evil than he could possibly have imagined. Those vile children with the sinister grins who asked him if he wanted to play were just as happy plotting his death.

He wheedled his way quietly back through the loft and descended the stairs. When he opened the door in the panelling, Steadman was waiting for him. The dog whined pathetically and lifted a paw to Stanley until he handed him the last morsel of meat.

Stanley stroked Steadman's head and scratched his chin. He had made a friend. But somewhere beneath the floorboards, the snake lay waiting for him.

When Stanley returned to his room he frantically covered every conceivable gap in the floor using anything he could find. Curled up in a tight ball on his bed, he looked up the Crow Snake in his book.

CROW SNAKE (Karasu-hebi)
Can grow to over six feet. Will curl up with

its tail vibrating in a similar manner to the rattlesnake and strike aggressively, with its mouth wide open.

Stanley couldn't possibly sleep. He had seen the snake's movement, sleek and swift. It would probably have reached his room even before he did. Perhaps he should rip up the floorboards and find it.

But what if he'd only *thought* he'd seen it? Maybe it wasn't coming to get him at all, and perhaps the girls had only made up their chant in jest.

He didn't know what to think. Eventually, his body couldn't hold out any longer and he drifted off into a heavy sleep. Soon he was dreaming.

As he dreamed, the dreadful verse rang in his head. He was walking out on the moor among the birds and through the long grass, but he could hear the girls' high voices singing, and the deep, listless tones of the double bass. He wandered near the lake and stood in the water as the cold wash lapped around his bare feet. He heard the rush of the reeds in the wind and as he stood, the wind in his face, the bulrushes began to rattle.

Stanley woke with a start. He knew what that rattle meant! He looked down and saw the coiled-up snake in front of him, poised to attack. His mind began to work at frantic speed. How could he move more quickly than the time it would take for the snake to strike?

The situation unfolded as if in slow motion. The snake's dreadful double head lunged upward at him, two open mouths revealing the sharp, poisoned fangs concealed within. Stanley ducked backward, banging his head on the headboard, clutching desperately at his bedclothes. The black snake got caught up in them, and thrashed wildly as Stanley wound the sheets round and round. Finally, he was sure that it was securely wrapped up inside them, and taking the broom from the corner of his room, he beat it and beat it until he was breathless and convinced that what lay inside was dead.

With the lifeless snake thrown to one side,

Stanley fell flat upon his mattress in exhaustion and didn't stir again until morning.

❦

When he finally awoke the next day, he cautiously unraveled the motionless snake from the sheets and placed it in a box in his cupboard.

There was a chance that this strange evidence might come in handy.

Stanley sat on the edge of his bed, thinking about the events of the day before. Berkeley jumped to the front of his mind. Where was the silver casket? Stanley thought back to the previous day down at the old candle shop and recalled that they had seen Berkeley down at the old Darkling place.

It made perfect sense. If Berkeley had wanted to keep the silver casket from Stanley, it would be a good idea to take it somewhere Stanley didn't even have access to.

Despite his long night, Stanley was up and about before Mrs. Carelli had even stirred. Only Victor was around, digging through more paperwork before he set off for the candle shop. "Just doing a little more research, lad," he said, lifting his head for a brief moment and looking over his half-moon glasses.

Stanley was the first to see that there was mail waiting on the mat. Two identical-looking envelopes, one for Mr. Darkling and one for Master Buggles. Stanley left the first and opened the second. It was from the village hall: a hearing would be held at the Crampton courtrooms in a week's time, to decipher ownership of the Hall.

He showed it to Victor, and decided he

would explain what had happened in the night. By the time Stanley had finished his tale, Victor was shocked. He jumped to his feet. "Where is this . . . snake?" he asked, in his most concerned voice. "Do you still have it?"

"It's still in my room," said Stanley.

"Bring it down, lad, and leave it with me. The more evidence we have, the better."

Stanley brought down the box containing the snake and promised that he would be back later. He sprinted down the path before the crows had awoken to his presence.

Down in the village the world was stirring. The fishermen had already left for the open sea. A smell of fresh bread drifted from the bakery, and doorways and windows were opening here and there.

Daisy trotted up behind Stanley. "You're up early!" she said, full of early-morning cheer. She was clutching a crusty loaf.

"So are you!" he answered.

"No, Stanley, I'm always up at this time. It's just that you're not around to see me! What's wrong?" she asked, sensing an uneasiness in his manner.

"The casket, Daisy. It's missing," he announced. "I know it was Berkeley who took it, and he was here yesterday, right? It's in the Darkling place, it must be. What do we do?"

Daisy accompanied Stanley to the old candle shop and they hung around outside it, looking over the rotted wooden shack that was the old Darkling place. Daisy's good knowledge of Crampton Rock was about to come into play again. It was something she'd found out long ago about the houses in the village: most had quick-access flaps or doorways built in to ensure a quick escape from *things in the night*, should the need arise.

It was likely that the Darkling house also had one, and if so it would be the best way in.

When Stanley and Daisy were sure that no one was looking, they crossed over to the old place to snoop around. Sure enough, behind the rickety wooden steps at the rear of the building there was a small square hatch with rusted hinges. Inside, a shaft of light shone on Stanley Buggles's inquisitive head; it broke a long spell of empty darkness.

Inside, the house was bare and unappealing.

A stale smell filled the air, and Stanley felt the urge to pull back the shutters, but Daisy stopped him. Dust particles swam around in the shafts of light that sneaked through the rotten wooded panels.

There was nothing here. Nothing but empty rooms, creaking floorboards, and damp walls, both upstairs and down. Old keys and scribbled notes lay on the windowsills. A small bowl of nails rested on the hearth, and a dusty black coat hung over one of the doors.

"I don't think it's here, Stanley," said Daisy. She peered out through a gap in the downstairs shutters.

Mr. Darkling was approaching the front door, with Annabelle at his side.

"Quick, Stanley!"

Their eyes scanned the room hastily,

searching for hiding places. Time was running out. The door creaked as Mr. Darkling stepped in and Annabelle followed.

"Arghhh . . . nothing!" cried Mr. Darkling.

"What is it, Father?" begged Annabelle.

"Still no mail," he muttered. "I am awaiting contact from my brother, important papers that I will need. But they are late. Perhaps tomorrow."

He walked into the front room and sniffed the air, his eyes shifting suspiciously from side to side.

"What is it *now*, Father?" asked Annabelle.

"Either that Buggles boy has been here, or his scent is jammed up my nose. But somehow I don't think he'll be bothering us anymore," he quipped. They turned and left, locking the door behind them.

Stanley and Daisy climbed down from

inside the chimney covered in soot.

"That was almost as close as last time," laughed Stanley.

"I can't handle all this," gasped Daisy. She was still holding the loaf of bread in her hand, but now it was black and looked as if it had been burned.

They left through the hatch, covering their tracks as they went. Daisy breathed in the fresh air, relieved to be out. But it was only a temporary relief.

"Hang on, Daisy. We need to go back in," announced Stanley.

"W-what for?"

"There was a telltale sign, and I almost missed it!" he began. When he'd stood on the ledge inside the chimney, he'd been staring into the little pot with the nails in it . . . and only half thinking.

"Explain, please!" said Daisy.

"I *bet* they're floorboard pins," Stanley said. He pushed his way back inside the hatch, and Daisy followed him reluctantly. "All we have to do is go back and find which ones were the creaking boards."

They separated and trod carefully through the house, Daisy checking the staircase first.

"Here," cried Stanley. "Down here." Daisy thundered down the shaky staircase to see Stanley trying to get his fingers into a gap between some boards, looking around for a tool to use. He picked up one of the nails from the bowl and forced it down the crack. Levering the edge of the board ever so slightly with his foot on the long nail, he slid his fingertips underneath and pulled upward.

A dust cloud choked their throats. When it had settled, they looked inside.

There, underneath the boards, thrown carelessly on its side, was the familiar lost casket. A beam of a smile crossed Stanley's face as he pulled it out and checked it over. Everything was still inside it, untouched. "No doubt Berkeley placed the casket there so that he might take a good look when he was able to return." Daisy said.

"No chance of that!" grinned Stanley.

As he and Daisy made their way back to the hatch, they heard someone climbing the steps to the front door. It was the postman; he had only just reached the bottom of the village. And now here he was, pushing a letter addressed to Edmund Darkling through the door.

Without pausing for thought, Stanley slipped it inside the casket, and they left.

Stanley didn't think it a good idea to wander through the village with the silver casket, as Berkeley had done, so they stole across the road to the candle shop. By now Victor was there, and they told him everything.

Vital
Evidence

For now, they decided to hide the silver casket in the shop. Victor was not entirely happy about this, fearing the old days of unsavory pirates darkening his door, but Stanley insisted that, for the moment, the place was not under observation.

Stanley was pleased with his find, but he was angry with Berkeley. Deep down he wanted to punch him in the nose, but Berkeley was half his size. And anyhow, he hoped to have revenge by taking the house back and sending Berkeley home. That *almost* made Stanley felt sorry for him.

In the safety of the candle shop, Stanley and Daisy sat in the back room with the silver casket proudly set on the tabletop. When Stanley had double-checked and triple-checked that all the pieces of the map were there, he studied the letter he'd taken from the house.

Daisy steamed open the envelope over a pan of boiling water, to make it look as if it had not been tampered with. Then she handed the letter to Stanley, who opened it to discover a short handwritten note.

My dear Edmund,

I trust you have made your move and laid claim to Candlestick Hall. I will send this to your house in case you are delayed, but by now you should be settled into the Darkling estate.

Shortly I will be with you, and once again the Darklings will rise. We set sail in a month's time. Both myself and my dear wife Marianne are eager to join you back in the family seat where we belong.

I hope our plans to be rid of the boy have been fully realized. As promised, I enclose the forged deeds which I have had scribed by an expert in these matters. Take great care with these. Such devious strategies do not come cheap. They have been made to look old, and so the parchment is torn and folded.

We will arrive in due course.
Meanwhile, I remain your affectionate
brother,

Ludwig

Daisy read the letter in shock. But Stanley grinned from ear to ear.

"Stanley!" exclaimed Daisy. "They plan to be rid of you for good, and in the meantime they've forged the deeds to your house— and you're sitting there smiling! Don't you understand, they're going to kill you!"

"Daisy, wait! Please, don't panic. Their plan has already failed. Last night I watched in secret as Mister Darkling laid a deadly plot. He charmed the dead body of a harmless mutated two-headed snake into a lethal living creature, then sent it under the boards toward my room. I captured it, and struck it until it was dead. Right now, Mister Darkling thinks I am lying lifeless on my bed. But the truth is that I am alive, and I have been handed the evidence that will seal the fate of the Darklings."

Victor's head appeared around the door. "What is all the excitement about?"

"Take a look, Victor," smiled Stanley.

Victor read the letter carefully. "Where did you get hold of this, Stanley?" he muttered. "We must present it in the court when the time comes."

They placed it carefully in the silver casket, then found a hiding place for the casket beneath the floor of the old candle shop, safe until it was needed again.

"In the meantime, the rest of our evidence is coming together nicely, Stanley," Victor informed him. "I spoke to the court on my way here about bringing Doctor Peebles in as a witness."

"Doctor Peebles! But what has Doctor Peebles got to do with any of this?" quizzed Stanley.

"Don't worry, lad," said Victor, smiling. "It will all become clear at the trial. You don't need to concern yourself with the details, not yet. I did some investigating of my own after you told me of the snake incident." He gave Stanley a look that said he knew what he was doing.

Stanley and Daisy headed out of the back entrance to make their way across the moor to visit the gypsies.

A strong smell of roasting meat drifted in their direction as they approached the camp, and they joined the group sitting around the fire. Warm drinks and cooked meat were handed among the families, as tales of long ago began to circulate. The dogs hung around greedily and stared at the meat with expectant faces. Stanley picked at the bones and fed them small chunks.

Phinn piped up. He wanted to tell Stanley

and Daisy the story of when the gypsies had arrived on the island, all those years ago. The two friends pricked up their ears and settled into comfortable positions.

"There is no place like the Rock. It is the center of the earth. Some say that once, the devil came here on horseback. That the hooves of his black mare were so fiery hot that they seared their shape into the very stones that lay across the land. Now, the grass grows so long and the wind blows so hard at that lofty point that no one would ever venture there and find out if it is true.

"When the travelers first came here, Stanley, there was nothing. Nothing but cold hard wind and the bleak moor. None of us was even born then: it was our fathers that came here and settled. They were free and happy and survived off the land. But their peace was short-lived.

"The curse of the wolf began to plague us. At first, we noticed howls at night, and the sheep were slowly disappearing. And then, before long, the dogs also. Of the ones that remained, all were three-legged, a sure sign of sinister struggles in the night.

"And then our first real loss. Wheelbarrow Wallace. Strong as an ox and our bravest warrior, taken one night while making his way home from the harbor. The first of many. They reckon the beast was badly wounded in the struggle that night."

"Like my brother, Ned," said Bartley. "He was taken one night, as he slept outside. Lucky for the wolf he wasn't awake," he chirped. "He would have torn it apart."

"And my Uncle Bill," said Phinn, jumping in. "Went one night to take out the beast with a shotgun. And all we found next day was the still-loaded weapon and a pile of bones with every bit of meat licked clean off!"

Daisy stared uneasily at the drumstick in her hand. Stanley secretly passed what was left of his to the dogs.

"We came back here when we discovered you had destroyed the beast, Stanley," continued Phinn. "You alone were the one brave enough to put the werewolf to rest for good with a silver bullet. We live in the hope that it will never return."

"There is no prospect of that," said Greta. "Here on the Rock and in other such strange places, darkness delivers the curse of the wolf. Not the fullness of the moon, nor any other such nonsense. It is sown in the soil of the land. The curse lives and breathes in the earth."

"Rubbish!" a woman cried out. "There are no wolves here, not anymore. They can't appear out o' nowhere."

"Remember what you say, sister," said Greta, with fire in her eyes. "Because tomorrow I will remind you of your words, and they may come back to haunt you."

Stanley and Daisy huddled nearer each other, spooked by the talk of the wolf's return. The younger children had heard too much and they were being put to bed as

Daisy urged Stanley that they should make their way back.

They decided to go down through the village and head up through the square. After all the wolf talk, they had no desire to cross the bleak moor in the oncoming darkness.

Stanley accompanied Daisy to the lighthouse, and then arrived back at the house much later. The crows descended as usual, only this time there seemed to be many more. Four or five flapped around his ankles, pecking and cawing, and another ten or maybe twelve were beating their wings about his head and scratching at his face. He fell to the ground, kicking helplessly at them until Victor came out and beat them away.

He picked himself up and they hurried inside. The whole house had stirred at the commotion, and everyone was assembled in the hallway.

The Darklings were dumbfounded to see Stanley. They had not had a glimpse of him all day, and Mr. Darkling had been hoping his sinister midnight plot had worked.

Stanley decided to say nothing about the snake. He would hang on to the story along with his evidence, and in the meantime pretend he knew nothing.

Mr. Darkling eyed him suspiciously, but he knew he could say nothing. His plan had failed and though he longed to know why and how, he knew he could not question the circumstances.

He had still not received the mail he awaited from his brother, and his claim to the house would look thin and weak without the forged deeds.

It had not been a good day for the Darkling cause.

Berkeley was glaring at Stanley too. He had been back down to the Darkling house earlier, only to discover that the silver casket was missing from beneath the floor. He had no proof, but he was sure that Stanley had reclaimed it.

Berkeley knew he could not ask for it; after all, he had stolen it in the first place.

"You think you're so clever, Stanley," he whined.

"Well, maybe I'm just a bit more clever than you,

Bark!" Stanley quipped, feeling pleased with himself.

"What did you call me?"

"Bark. It's your new name. Seeing as how Victor thinks you are a little dog," Stanley grinned.

Berkeley deadened his eyes to Stanley, and beckoned his trusty hound. "Kill, Steadman. Kill."

Steadman went pounding over to Stanley, smelled the meat from the gypsy camp on his hands, and licked him lovingly until an annoyed Berkeley pulled him away.

"How did you do that, Stanley?"

"Do what?" Stanley asked innocently.

"Make him *like* you. How did you make him *like* you like that?"

"As you say, Bark, I'm clever! Woof woof," Stanley shouted as Berkeley turned to leave the room.

Berkeley edged
back inside the
door and stared
hard at Stanley. And then he
growled menacingly at him, baring his short
pointed teeth and turning up his little snub
nose. He held his hands out like claws.

Stanley would have been frightened, had
he not been so amused. "Run along now, Bark.
There's a good boy."

"Stanley, you make me so *cross*. You think
you're big and clever and you never, ever,
EVER play with me," said Berkeley, and he
ran out of the room in tears.

And Stanley felt a trickle of guilt run
through him.

Could it be true that all that this sinister
little boy *really* wanted, more than anything
else, was someone to be his friend?

11

Silence in Court

The courthouse stood in one corner of the village, overlooking the square, and there were a series of long rooms at the top of one of the buildings which gave a good view out to sea.

A group of people was milling around, waiting to be allowed in. Stanley's nerves drummed around inside him, and he felt fluttering in his stomach.

Miss Spoonbill was present, along with
two older gentlemen, one thin and one fat.
A Mr. Barker and a Mr. Rook.
Mr. Barker would act on behalf of
his client Mr. Darkling and Mr. Rook,

respectively would act on behalf of Master Buggles. Their faces looked old and grumbly. Perhaps they wouldn't like the idea of a young boy with his own mansion, thought Stanley.

There were court officials everywhere, and Stanley recognized them as people from the village dressed in black robes and strange pieces of headwear. The court made it clear that they were not allowed to greet Stanley, but one man, a local fisherman, gave him a knowing wink and he felt spurred on by it.

Finally, they filed through the door and sat in high-backed chairs around a table that ran the length of the room. At one end were the people who Stanley knew must be the jury, the people who would make the final decision. He knew there were faces from the village, but he tried not to look.

Then in walked a small, frail man, who

appeared to be almost lost under his robes. Everyone was instructed to stand up for Judge Angus Bumble, and when he sat down they all followed his example. Judge Bumble would oversee the proceedings and have the final say.

The Darklings bunched up opposite Stanley, the children sitting still and silent. Berkeley had been given strict orders to keep himself under control. He, Annabelle, and Olive fixed their stares on Stanley, never seeming to blink or move.

Miss Spoonbill opened the session with a long speech that Stanley couldn't quite understand. Instead he scribbled a picture of a small dog and held it up discreetly, but so that only Berkeley could see it across the table.

Maybe it was the nervousness in the courtroom or perhaps something else, but for the first time, Stanley saw Berkeley break into a chuckle. The chuckle became a laugh, and then the laugh brought down a clout from Mrs. Darkling on the back of Berkeley's head.

"Silence in court while the judge blows his nose," came a loud voice. Judge Angus Bumble fumbled in his robes, took out a handkerchief resembling a tablecloth, and began to clear his snout noisily.

It was too much for Berkeley. His fit of giggles had begun, and the nose-blowing incident only made it worse.

Stanley was stronger. He knew a fit of

giggles would not help win
the court's favor, and so
he held on to his resolve,
concentrating his thoughts
on what lay ahead.

"Let us begin," said the
judge when he had folded
his hanky neatly away.

Mr. Darkling spoke first.
He told of his family history on the Rock.
How he had spent his childhood at the
Darkling estate, and how it had been taken
from his parents by Admiral Swift, a cunning
and merciless buccaneer. And that the
paperwork to prove his claim was on its way.

"You make a feeble case, Mister Darkling,"
suggested Mr. Rook. "Without any form of
evidence, you accuse Admiral Swift of piracy
and of the theft of your home. If you have

paperwork that proves your case, it should be present in court."

"But the Hall is still filled with our things. My family name is written in stone upon its very walls," claimed Mr. Darkling, gritting his teeth and staring at Stanley.

"I'm afraid," continued Mr. Rook, "that only serves to confirm it was built for Brice Darkling. It gives you no entitlement to the estate."

"But the boy," Mr. Darkling growled. "He is not fit to run such a place. He has brought nothing but trouble here since he came. Only recently, the whole place was swarming with pirates."

"Nonsense!" burst out Mrs. Carelli. "We've always lived in fear of piracy out here on the Rock, long before the boy came here. 'Tis ridiculous to claim he is responsible."

It was time for Victor to bring forward the evidence on behalf of Stanley. He was armed with piles of papers and a small box with a flimsy lid.

"When you're ready," said Mr. Barker. He had a low, gentle voice and a kind smile.

Victor joined Stanley.

"Here is the proof of purchase regarding the sale of Darkling Hall to Admiral Swift by Edmund Darkling's father. Here is the proof of Stanley's family connection to Admiral Swift, bearing in mind he left no will and that the laws of Crampton Rock entitle the youngest family member to the estate. And, of course, here are the deeds belonging to Stanley Buggles for the presently named Candlestick Hall estate."

"Thank you, Mister Carelli. Thank you. I think that is enough to be going on with. Mister Darkling, is there anything you wish to respond with at this point?"

"I wish to postpone these proceedings," cried out Mr. Darkling. "I am still awaiting vital evidence that will prove my claim."

"I think we have the evidence that Mister Darkling speaks of!" suggested Victor. All eyes fell on him.

"Continue," said Judge Bumble.

Victor read out the letter from Mr. Darkling's brother Ludwig that explained the plans to forge the deeds to the Hall and, much worse, to be rid of young Stanley. The whole courtroom gasped in surprise.

"Silence in court, please," Mr. Barker called.

"Murderers!" It was Bartley shouting and shaking his fists.

Mr. Barker got to his feet. "And how did you come by this information, Mister Carelli?"

"Well . . . we took it, sir. We took it from the house," struggled Victor.

"You took it from *which* house?" continued the investigation.

"From . . . the Darkling house, sir!" Victor admitted.

Gasps went up. The court was stirring with "ooh's" and "aah's" as Stanley jumped to his feet.

"It was me, sir. I took it from the Darkling place. I shouldn't have . . . but . . . but I was desperate to get hold of the truth, sir!"

"Sit down please, Master Buggles," asked Mr. Barker.

He waited a moment, and when Stanley had composed himself, he continued.

"Do you mean to tell me that in collecting your evidence

for this court, you broke into a house in the village and stole mail belonging to someone other than yourself?"

"Yes . . . sir. Although I didn't really see it that way, it's just that—"

But he was stopped in his tracks.

"Mister Barker, am I right in thinking that Master Buggles is explaining that he obtained his evidence by illegal means?" questioned Judge Bumble.

"Yes, sir, I think that is the general idea of what he is explaining."

"Then you must remind him that this court does not accept any form of evidence acquired in such a manner."

"Of course, sir. Yes I will." Mr. Barker repeated this to the court and instructed the jury that they should not take this evidence into account.

"Could we have the next piece of evidence please?" asked Mr. Rook.

Unshaken by the events so far, Victor took the lid from the box and lifted the dead body of the snake on to the table. There were more gasps as Stanley explained what had happened.

"Will you please be quiet. I will have no choice but to adjourn this court if we cannot view the evidence under civilized circumstances . . . Thank you," said Judge Bumble, as the noise dissolved into a whispering hush.

"Mister Darkling, perhaps you wish to comment on the presence of a snake in the boy's room, and your plot to be rid of him?" suggested Mr. Rook.

Mr. Darkling stared hard at Mr. Rook. "I know nothing of this," he claimed. "It is irrelevant. The house is full of such curiosities."

"And you claimed earlier that all of those deadly objects are yours?" smiled Mr. Rook.

Again, Mr. Darkling was lost for an answer. A whisper passed among several court officials.

"Could we call a Doctor Peebles, please?" asked Mr. Barker. A stringy-framed man strolled aimlessly into the room and made his way to the front. He was carrying a large case and seemed to be blissfully unaware of what was going on or why he was there at all.

"Doctor Peebles," began Mr. Barker, "could you tell the court what you do here on the island?"

"Well, yes, of course. I'm the village doctor here, sir," he said, peering over his half-moon glasses, his back hunched up as if it couldn't bear the weight of his head.

"Not much call for anything serious here on the Rock, I wouldn't have thought," suggested Mr. Barker.

"Well, no, but the fishermen often come to me with strange bites and stings after a day out on the ocean. There are thousands of unknown toxins in those waters, sir! It's quite common for me to deal with those."

"And how do you go about dealing with them? Where do you get your remedies?" Mr. Barker questioned further.

"Well, I have a supplier of antidotes," the doctor explained.

"And what are these antidotes made up of?" pressed Mr. Barker.

"We use snake venoms, sir," Dr. Peebles explained. A whispered, knowing rumble ran around the jury box.

"Quiet, please. Do continue, doctor. Do

tell us who your snake expert is," asked Mr. Barker.

"Well, it's Mister Darkling, of course. He is a snake breeder and an excellent toxicologist."

The excited whisper grew louder, and again the crowd was told to hush.

"And what of the snake we asked you to examine? What did you make of that?" continued Mr. Barker.

"It was a Black Crow Snake, sir. Not known to be poisonous, but it had been mutated, do you understand? It had been altered to carry a poison. Typical of Mister Darkling's work, sir, he is a genius I must say, I—"

"Yes, thank you, Doctor Peebles. That will be all," finished Mr. Barker. The jury members were on their feet. The spectators' cries rang out again.

"Murderer! Send him down!"

"Silence in court." Out came the large handkerchief again, and the judge cleared his nostrils before he began to speak.

"We are veering away from the case here. If you feel we have clearly established a false claim upon Candlestick Hall, you must reflect this in your judgment. If you feel the case is unclear, you must be sure to set aside your emotions and face the facts. Make your decision wisely. The incident with the snake must not influence your decision over the ownership of the Hall. A separate hearing is likely to follow regarding attempted murder. And do not forget that any evidence gathered under dubious circumstances is deemed irrelevant.

"Let us adjourn so that you may make your decision."

A tense period of waiting followed. Stanley shuffled in his seat, his palms sweating.

Finally, the court assembled itself back into position.

"Jury, are you ready to give your decision?" asked Mr. Rook.

A small round man with spectacles stood up for the jury. "We are," he announced.

"And what have you decided?" continued Mr. Rook.

The man read a short statement from a scrap of paper.

"We, the jury, have together decided that the evidence produced by Buggles and Carelli cannot be recognized and is therefore not part of this case."

Stanley's heart sank into his stomach.

"Master Buggles is new to the island and as the court is aware, all newcomers have to be officially accepted by the community, should they wish to stay. It is not in the interests of the Rock that such criminal activity occurs and as a jury we are naturally swayed by it."

Stanley sank farther into his chair. A feeling of great shame washed over him, and the realization that he had put everything at risk by entering the Darkling home hit him hard.

"But there is nothing to suggest that the Darkling family has any legal claim on the estate presently known as Candlestick Hall," continued the man. "Their attachment is purely emotional and therefore by residing within its grounds they are trespassing on the estate belonging to Stanley Buggles."

Gasps of relief came from Stanley's side of the room.

"Silence in the court," came the voice of Mr. Barker. "Judge Bumble will now speak."

All eyes were fixed on Judge Bumble, bent over in his seat at the head of the room.

"Edmund Darkling, you have seven days to gather your belongings and return with your family to your home in the village. This court recognizes Stanley Buggles's claim to the Candlestick estate.

"I understand, Master Buggles, that in a moment of desperation you did something that was foolish. May I remind you that in future you should wait until invited before stepping through the door of any property.

"Regarding the seriousness of Edmund Darkling's attempt on Stanley Buggles's life, further enquiries shall be made.

"This court is now ended."

Judge Bumble stepped down from his perch and left the room.

A fevered excitement surrounded Stanley

and Victor. And at the same time a black cloud hung over the Darklings as they gathered themselves together.

The two sides collided in the doorway as they left the courtroom. Berkeley ran out into the street, trying to make Stanley chase him. He had no real understanding of the seriousness of the situation. Mrs. Darkling rushed past, tears running down her face, but Mr. Darkling stopped and turned to Stanley.

"You will live to regret this, young Buggles. You haven't seen the last of me."

12

Back to Candlestick

As they walked through the village, Stanley caught sight of Daisy waiting for them. Mrs. Carelli had asked her to stay in the Hall during the hearing. She hadn't trusted the Darklings, fearing that they might arrange some sinister goings-on while they were all out.

Daisy was dancing anxiously around from

toe to toe. But when Stanley was close enough
for her to see his face, she knew immediately
that the news was good.

As they neared the Hall, the crows were
making a most terrible din. They were much
louder than they had ever been before.
Swooping down, they seemed to be making

a last-ditch attempt to be rid of Stanley and the Carellis. A huge black swarm of beating wings flocked around them, stabbing at their faces with sharp beaks and clawing feet. Loose feathers filled the air. Stanley, Victor, and Mrs. Carelli batted them off, flailing with injured hands.

"Edmund, stop it. It serves no purpose. Stop them, now." Mrs. Darkling's voice sounded from the foot of the pathway.

Mr. Darkling let out a strange, howling cry. Every single bird stopped and swooped back onto the roof. The victims nursed their injured faces as they struggled in through the front door.

At the Hall an awkward period followed. The Darklings were of course extremely unhappy at the jury's decision, and they knew that sooner or later Mr. Darkling would face the court again for his murderous attempts. Meanwhile, Stanley rejoiced at the good news and his side of the house couldn't help but erupt with joy.

"Daisy, now we can spend our time working out what the map shows," said Stanley excitedly. They were sitting on the bare floor of Stanley's room with drinks and cakes, poring over the instructions.

"I was looking it over while you were in court," Daisy said, "and I think there's something odd about the map."

Daisy was right. The path seemed to wind in twisting, turning steps through what they were sure was the village square.

"To go from one end of the village to the other, you would go in a straight line. There's no need to wind this way and that," said Stanley.

"Yes, but hang on," started Daisy, "this map is old. Very old. It goes back to when this place was different, when great hills and giant rocks stood here, before there were houses. At one time the way along here might have gone through a winding pass surrounded by huge trees."

"Daisy, how do you do it?" laughed Stanley. "I would never have thought of that in a million years."

Right then, a shuffling, knocking sound came from outside the bedroom door.

Stanley opened it quickly and found the Darkling children taking turns peering in through the keyhole.

"What do you want?" he asked.

"Berkeley has made you something, Stanley," Annabelle and Olive said at the same time.

"What . . . what is it?" he asked, eyeing it suspiciously.

"Something to say thank you for letting us stay," they all replied.

Berkeley handed Stanley a painting, smeared with handprints, of something four-legged.

"Oh . . . er . . . that's . . . nice," said Stanley awkwardly. "What is it?"

"It's Steadman," said Berkeley, as if Stanley should have known immediately.

"Of course it is," Stanley answered. " It's fantastic! Thank you so much."

"We know you like him really, so we thought you might want something to remember him by."

The familiar *click click click* of Steadman's feet sounded across the wooden floor, and he appeared beside them, wagging his tail.

Stanley patted his head and stroked the underside of his chin. Secretly, Stanley had developed a growing admiration of Steadman, and now Steadman loved him back. He was just a big old softy.

Daisy exchanged surprised looks with the Darkling children. Berkeley shrugged his shoulders and chuckled.

"Come on," Stanley said, and Steadman and

the children trotted down the staircase after him. Stanley sneaked quickly into the pantry and pinched a handful of meat, feeding it to Steadman.

Mrs. Darkling spotted that they were all together. "Come on!" she shrieked from the top of the stairs. "Back up here at once, children. Steadman, here boy!"

"I'll see you soon, Stanley Boogles," said Berkeley.

"Buggles. It's Buggles'" corrected Stanley.

"BOOGLES!" insisted Berkeley, and he chuckled, revealing his sharp grin.

"All right, BARK. I'll see you later," Stanley smiled.

"Woof woof," said Berkeley.

Steadman raised a final paw to Stanley before leaving, and Mrs. Darkling pierced him with her tiny black eyes before slamming their door.

"Well, well, Stanley. Things seem to have turned out for the best." It was the pike, managing to make himself heard from his place on the wall.

"You even managed to get the hound to eat out of your hand. Most impressive, Stanley. Darkness is lifting from the house already. I couldn't have stood that dreadful boy a moment longer."

"Yes, I know," said Stanley. "It has been quite a strain. But I almost feel sorry for them now that I've seen the house they must go back to. It is a dreadful place, rundown and ramshackle. I hope I never have to go there again. "

"Oh, you'll change your mind about that, I'm sure," said the pike. "The old Darkling place is not as insignificant as you might have thought."

"What do you mean by that?" asked Stanley, but the pike had decided, as he often did, that he was not going to say any more.

The Final Twist

The next morning, the Darklings were preparing to leave. Immediately, Stanley noticed the crows flocking from the roof and heading down into the village, where he presumed they were returning to the old place. The beating and flapping of a thousand wings, the cawing and crowing of every beak made a terrible noise. But it was as if a dark cloud had lifted from over the house, and the sun was allowed to shine on them again.

The Darklings gathered their things and began to load them back into the old cart.

"I don't want to watch them leaving," Stanley said to Victor and Mrs. Carelli. "It feels ill-mannered, as if I'm gloating. Come on," he said, turning to Daisy and adding in a whisper, "Let's go and investigate. Can we go over to the candle shop, Victor?"

"Of course, lad," Victor said, and handed him the door key from the piece of string tied about his neck. "'I'll be bobbing along myself soon."

And as the Darkling family moved their meager belongings out of the house, Stanley and Daisy headed into the village, the map concealed in Daisy's pocket. They knew that when they next returned to Candlestick Hall it would be back to normal and they would be at peace.

❦

It took Stanley and Daisy only an hour to decipher the map. They sat in the candle shop again, the map out on the table, and studied it hard until they agreed that they had understood it in the same way. They left the shop and traced their way back to the starting point, which they were sure was at the harbor, and measured their way carefully along the route described on the map.

It meandered here and there, twisting and turning, and they imagined passing through the winding route of trees that had once stood there.

Then it took them away from the village and they headed back toward the moor, past the village hall. Stanley pushed ahead, climbing the rocks.

"Wait!" said Daisy. "We turn right here, under the old watchtower."

"But that takes us back into the village," Stanley argued. "We'll be back at the candle shop."

Daisy shrugged her shoulders. "Check it," she said. So he did.

"You're right, Daisy. You're definitely right," he agreed, and they veered back into the village.

"We're almost there, Stanley. There's not far to go."

Stanley and Daisy looked around them. The cobbled streets were alive with people.

"This could prove to be very difficult," said Stanley, scratching his head.

"Come on," said Daisy. "We have to find where it leads to!"

Stanley paced the way that Daisy read out to him, measuring the distances with his bow-legged stride. Daisy walked behind him, her head down, not looking at what lay up ahead. "Stanley, do you realize that we are about to uncover something very ancient and very, very valuable?" muttered Daisy. "This map is so old it is almost falling apart in my hands. You have no idea what this could mean. Fame and fortune. Untold riches," she laughed. "Now, just ten more paces north of where you are now, Stanley, and that's it. X marks the spot, as they say."

"Oh . . . oh dear," said Stanley in a troubled tone. "This is it, Daisy. This is where our precious treasure lies!"

"What?" asked Daisy. "What is it?" But as she looked up, she knew. Stanley was standing directly in front of the old Darkling place. The shutters banged in the wind and the flock of crows stared down at them, cawing and flapping their shrouds.

"It's *here*," Stanley said, looking right at her. "It's right here, where this building stands."

And just then they heard the sound of rolling cartwheels behind them: the Darklings, returning with all their belongings. They pulled up to the front of their old home. Edmund Darkling unlocked its worn and weathered entrance and watched his family step inside. He gave Stanley Buggles a cold, hard glance, and then he closed his door on Crampton Rock.

Stanley turned to Daisy. A lump welled up in his throat. "I thought all our troubles were over," he said. "But somehow Daisy, I think they've only just begun."